SPECTRUM READERS

EXPLORE!

Rain Forests

By Lisa Kurkov

Carson-Dellosa
Publishing

SPECTRUM®

An imprint of Carson-Dellosa Publishing, LLC
P.O. Box 35665
Greensboro, NC 27425-5665

© 2014, Carson-Dellosa Publishing, LLC. Except as permitted under the United States Copyright Act, no part of this publication may be reproduced, stored, or distributed in any form or by any means (mechanically, electronically, recording, etc.) without the prior written consent of Carson-Dellosa Publishing, LLC. Spectrum is an imprint of Carson-Dellosa Publishing, LLC.

carsondellosa.com

Printed in the USA. All rights reserved.
ISBN 978-1-4838-0127-8

01-002141120

All around the world, tropical rain forests can be found close to the equator.
They are hot and wet all year long.
It rains about 80 inches each year here!
Tree and plant growth is so thick that most sunlight never reaches the ground.
Warm, moist tropical rain forests make habitats for thousands of plants and animals.

Earth's Rain Forests

Earth's largest rain forest is found in South America along the Amazon River. The Amazon River follows a path about 4,000 miles long—longer than the United States from coast to coast!

Tropical rain forests also grow in Asia, Australia, and Africa.

The average temperature is 77°F. It rains here nearly every day.

Fascinating Facts

- English explorer Ed Stafford walked the entire length of the Amazon River in 2010.

- It can take as long as ten minutes for rain to drip to the ground in a rain forest. That's how thick the leaf cover is!

emergent layer

canopy

understory

forest floor

Rain Forest Layers

Rain forests have four layers, or stories.
The forest floor is the first layer.
Shade from huge plants makes it dark.
The low-light understory comes next.
It is home to jaguars and tree frogs.
Most animals live in the next layer, the leafy canopy.
At the very top of the tall trees is the hot, windy emergent layer.

Fascinating Facts

- Scientists study the canopy using hot air balloons, cranes, gliders, and walkways.

- The world's largest flower, the rafflesia, grows on the forest floor. It can measure 10 feet across!

Plant Life

Thousands of tree species flourish in the rain forest.

About 750 different types of trees can be found in a four-mile patch of forest.

Rain forest trees must grow quickly to reach the sunlight.

Some are more than 150 feet tall—almost as tall as the Statue of Liberty!

Fascinating Facts

- Monkeys swing on the long vines of the liana plant. The vines help them get around the forest.

- Many rain forest plants have not been discovered or named yet!

Poison Dart Frog

Poison dart frogs live on the forest floor. Even though one frog is only an inch or two in length, its skin has enough venom to kill ten humans!

Poison dart frogs use sticky tongues to hunt for bugs in rotting leaves. Anteaters, turtles, and scorpions also eat insects they find on the rain forest floor.

Fascinating Facts

- Poison dart frogs can be blue, yellow, red, black, green, copper, or gold. The bright colors signal danger.

- Some rain forest people put the frogs' toxin on the tips of darts.

Leafcutter Ant

Fungi, worms, and beetles thrive on the warm, damp rain forest floor.
Leafcutter ants live here, too.
These amazing ants slice off large pieces of plants and leaves and carry them back to their underground nests.
The ants chew up the leaves and use the pulp to help grow a fungus they can eat.

Fascinating Facts

- More than five million leafcutter ants live in a single nest.

- Leafcutter ants can carry about 50 times their own weight!

Emerald Tree Boa

Emerald tree boas hang from trees in the forest understory.
Their bright green color helps them hide in the green leaves.
This sneaky snake wraps around a branch and waits for a rat, bird, or other small creature to come close.
It grabs the animal and squeezes with its powerful body.

Fascinating Facts

- The green anaconda also lives in the understory. This snake can grow 30 feet long, almost as long as a school bus!

- A jaguar's spots help it blend in with the spotted light of the understory.

Orangutan

Reddish-brown orangutans live in the rain forests of Southeast Asia.
Like squirrel monkeys and lemurs, they make their home in the canopy layer.
Here, orangutans find plenty of leaves and fruit to eat.
They are also safe from predators.
Orangutans are shy and smart.
They use leaves to make cups for drinking water.

Fascinating Facts

- The name *orangutan* means "person of the forest."
- Baby orangutans stay with their mothers until they are at least six years old.

Hornbill

Hornbills also live in the canopy.
They nest in holes in trees.
The male makes a mud wall over the
opening, and the female and eggs stay
safe inside.
Many other birds, like the toucan, also
make their homes in the canopy.
It is a safe place for tropical birds to feed
on the fruit they love.

Fascinating Facts

- Hornbills and toucans are known for their large beaks, which are light and hollow.

- Hornbills fly over the forest, dropping waste that contains seeds. This helps new plants spread.

19

Macaw

Macaws are large parrots that live high up in the emergent layer.
Their calls, squawks, and screams echo through the treetops.
These bright, noisy birds stand almost three feet tall—that's the height of a human toddler.
Other flying animals such as bats, harpy eagles, and butterflies also make their homes in the windy emergent layer.

Fascinating Facts

- Macaws make good partners—they mate for life.
- Macaws use their large, powerful beaks to break into nuts and seeds.

Rain Forest Products

Did you know that you use products from rain forests every day?

Bananas, coffee, cinnamon, cashew nuts, cocoa, and vanilla are just a few forest foods you may find in your kitchen.

Brazil's rubber trees produce latex, which is used to make rubber for boots, tires, doormats, and other items.

Even your houseplants may have first been discovered in the rain forest.

Fascinating Facts

- Sap from the tropical chicle tree is used to make chewing gum.

- Oils in shampoo, lotion, and perfume often come from rain forest plants.

Medicines

Many life-saving medicines come from rain forests.

Scientists have found many rare and useful chemicals in rain forest plants. They use these chemicals to make medicines that treat cancer, arthritis, diabetes, and other diseases.

Many other cures may still be hiding in rain forests!

Fascinating Facts

- Seventy percent of plants that can be used to treat cancer are found *only* in rain forests.

- The rosy periwinkle plant is used to treat a type of cancer called *leukemia*.

Native Peoples

Native tribes of people have lived in rain forests for thousands of years. Their members know how to use what the forest has to offer. Their way of life depends on the forest. It provides food, shelter, and medicine. In return, the people take care of the forests.

Fascinating Facts

- Many rain forest peoples move to a new patch of forest every few years. Cleared trees have a chance to grow back.

- When rain forests disappear, trees and animals lose their lives. Cultures and traditions are lost, too.

Disappearing Forests

Rain forest land is cleared every day.
Often, cleared land is used for farming.
People mine for gold in some areas.
In other places, timber companies cut
down trees for wood.
Plants and animals depend on each other
in a rain forest.
The loss of one species is tied to others.

Fascinating Facts

- Trees take in carbon dioxide, a gas that traps heat. With fewer rain forest trees, the planet may keep getting warmer.

- Floods happen more often in areas where trees have been cleared.

Wild Places

Rain forests are some of the most beautiful, wild places left on Earth. Many rare plants and animals that live here are found nowhere else. What exciting future discoveries will be made in rain forests? What medicines or cures will be found? How many species are still mysteries? Rain forests hold some of our planet's most interesting secrets.

Fascinating Facts

- More than half of the world's animals are found in rain forests.

- Every second, we lose a patch of rain forest about the size of a football field.

EXPLORE! Rain Forests
Comprehension Questions

1. About how much rain do tropical rain forests receive each year?

2. What are the four layers of a rain forest?

3. Why do most rain forest trees grow quickly?

4. What do poison dart frogs eat?

5. Why do you think fewer plants and animals live on the forest floor?

6. Why is the emerald tree boa green?

7. What foods do orangutans find in the rain forest canopy?

8. Why does the male hornbill make a mud wall over the opening to its nest?

9. Name three rain forest products.

10. Why are rain forest plants important in the medical world?